The Moon

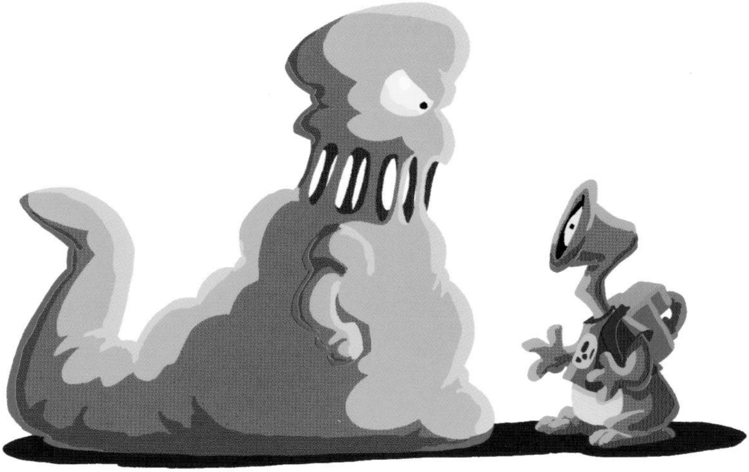

Illustrated by Raymond McGrath

Rigby

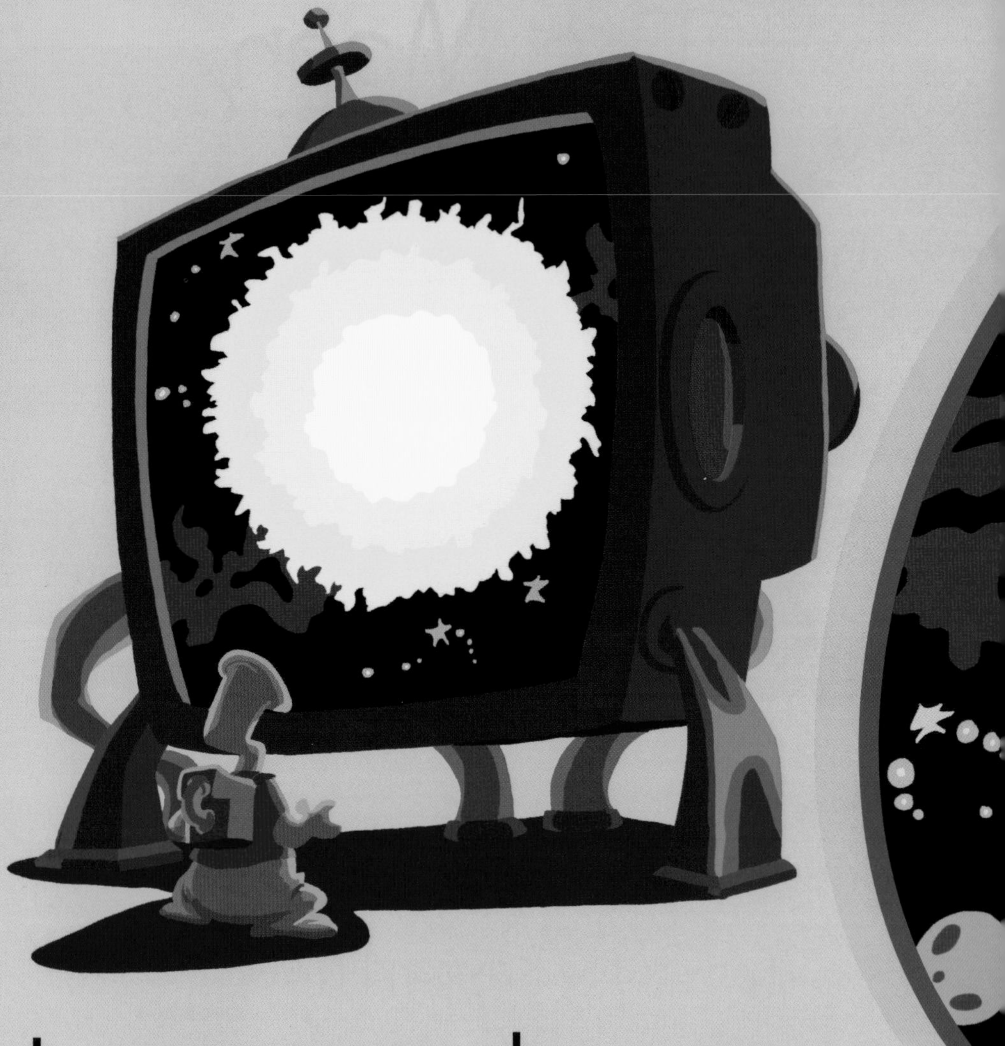

I can see the sun.

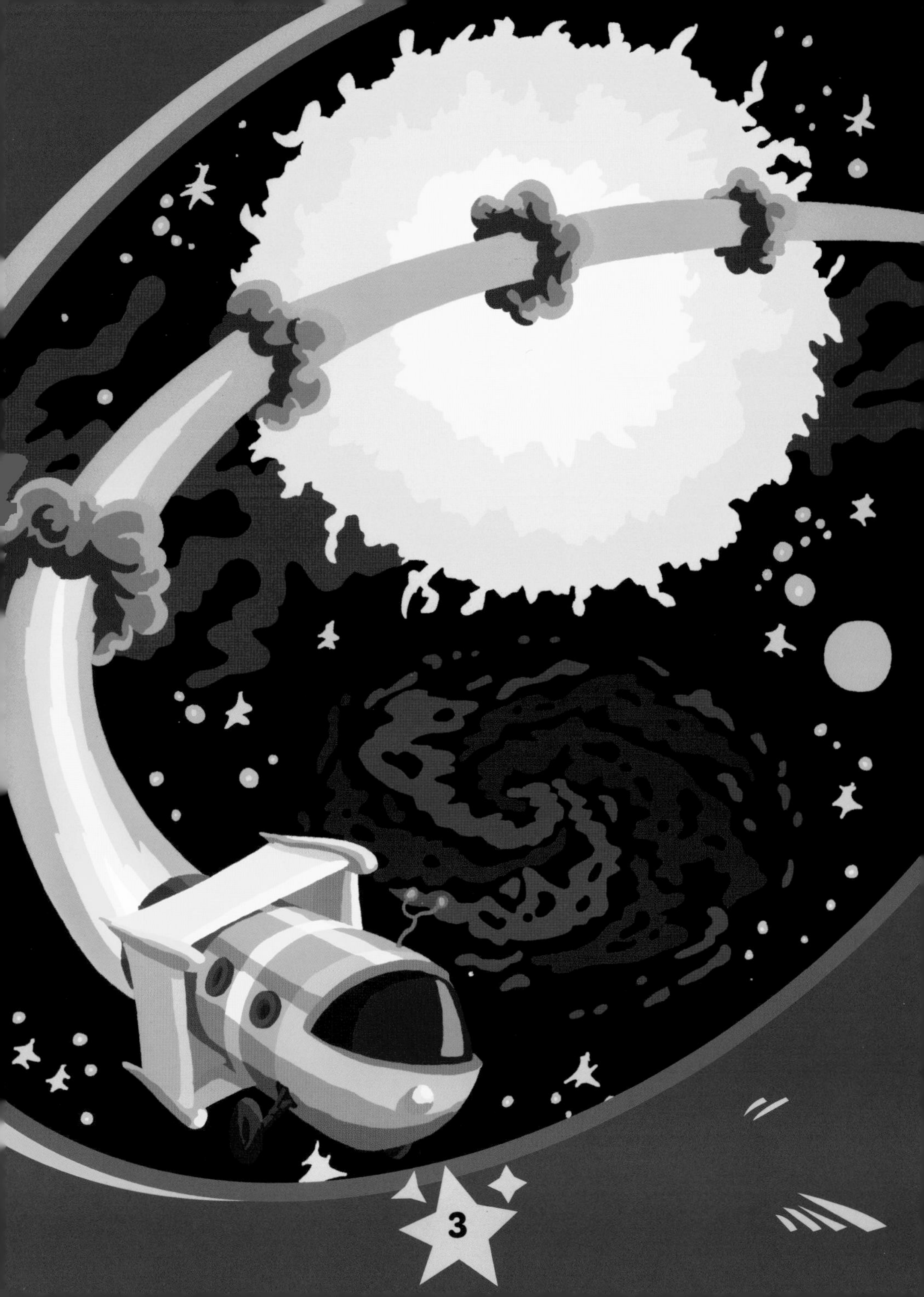

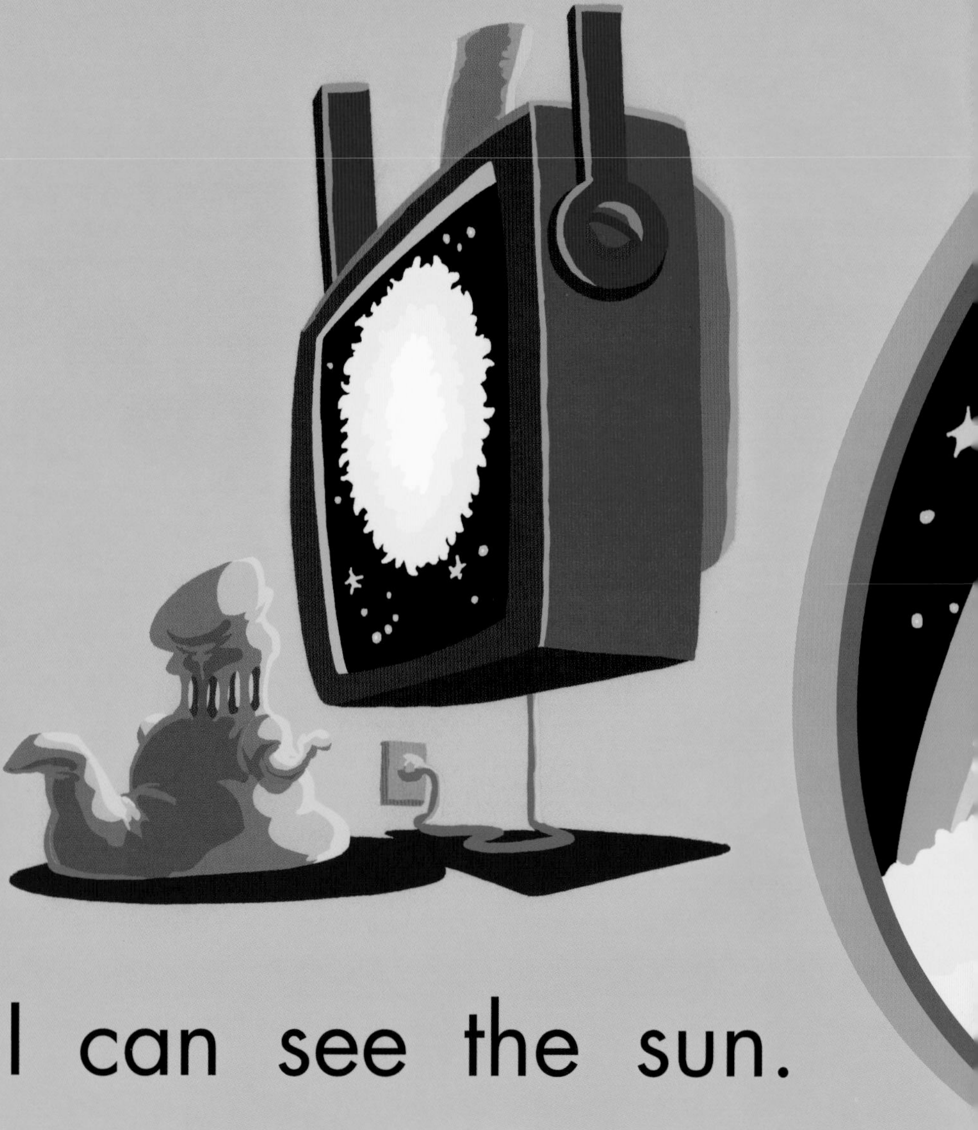

I can see the sun.

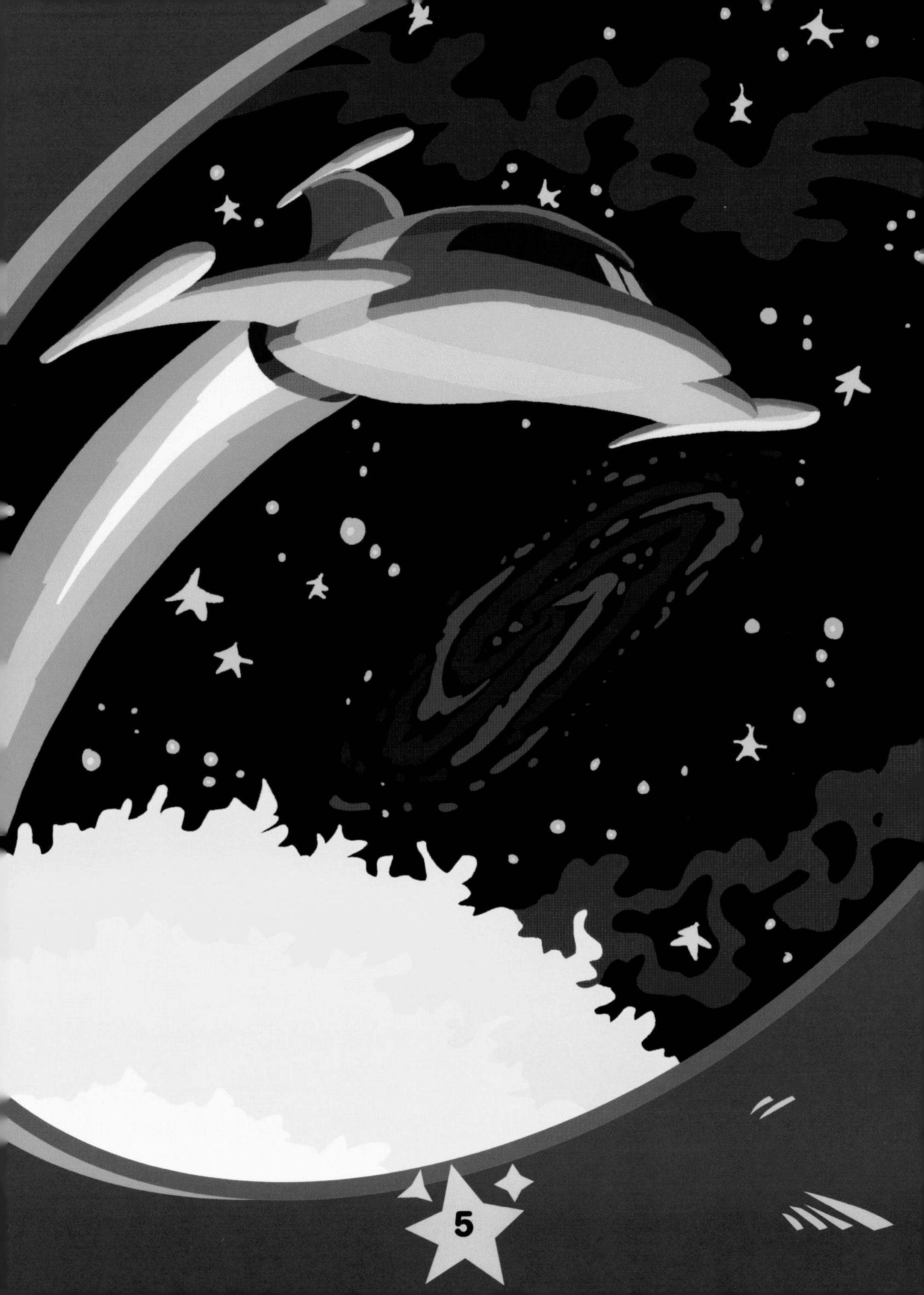

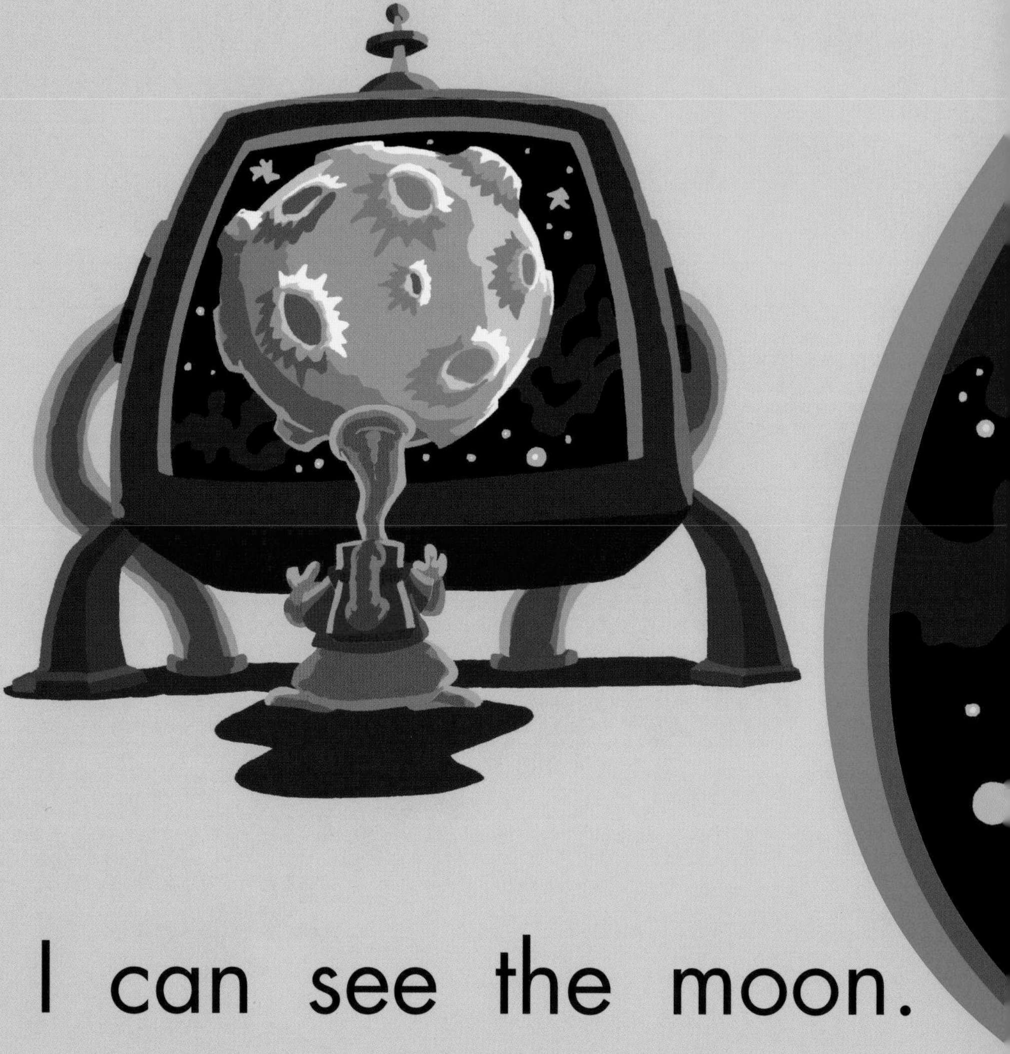

I can see the moon.

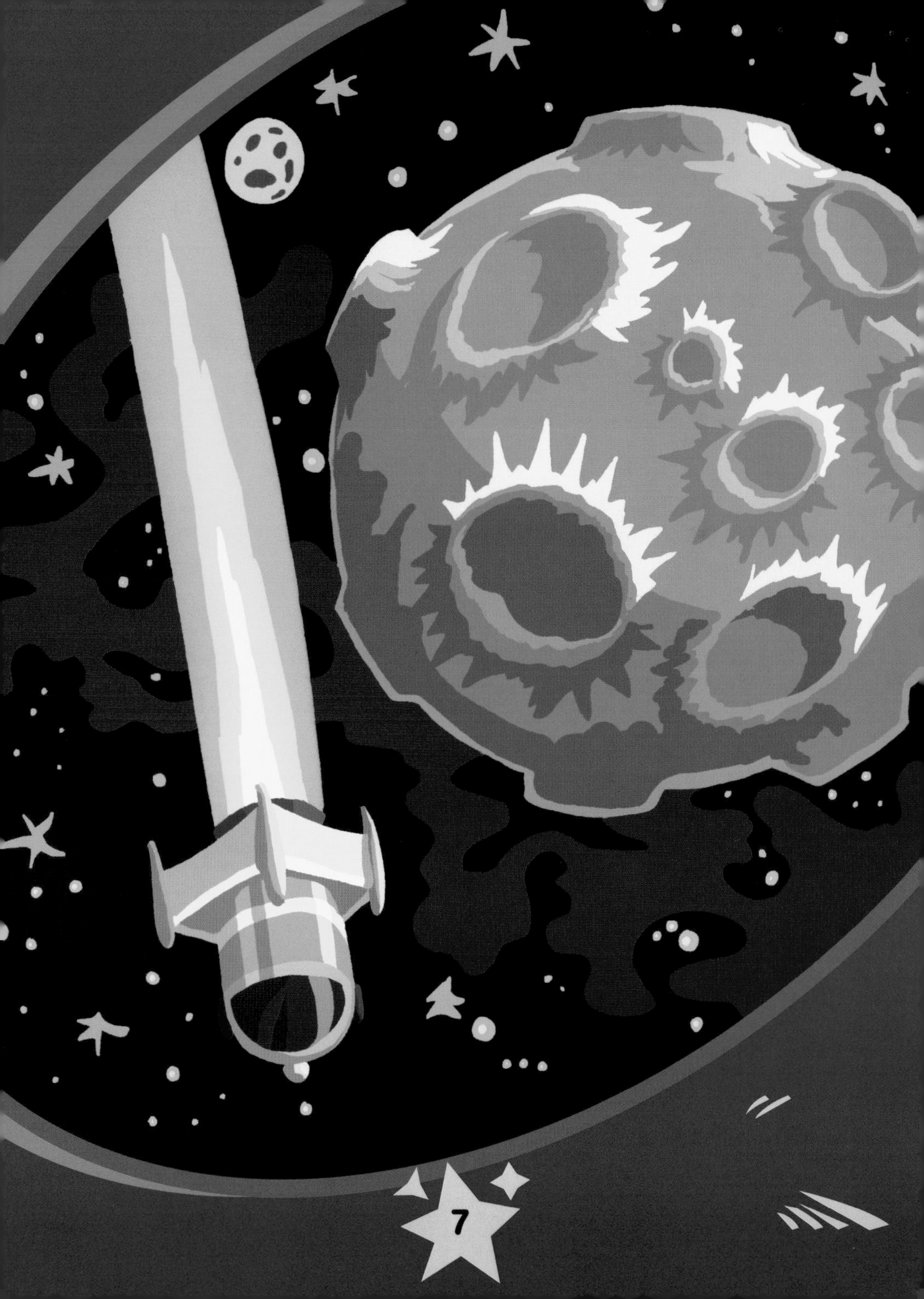

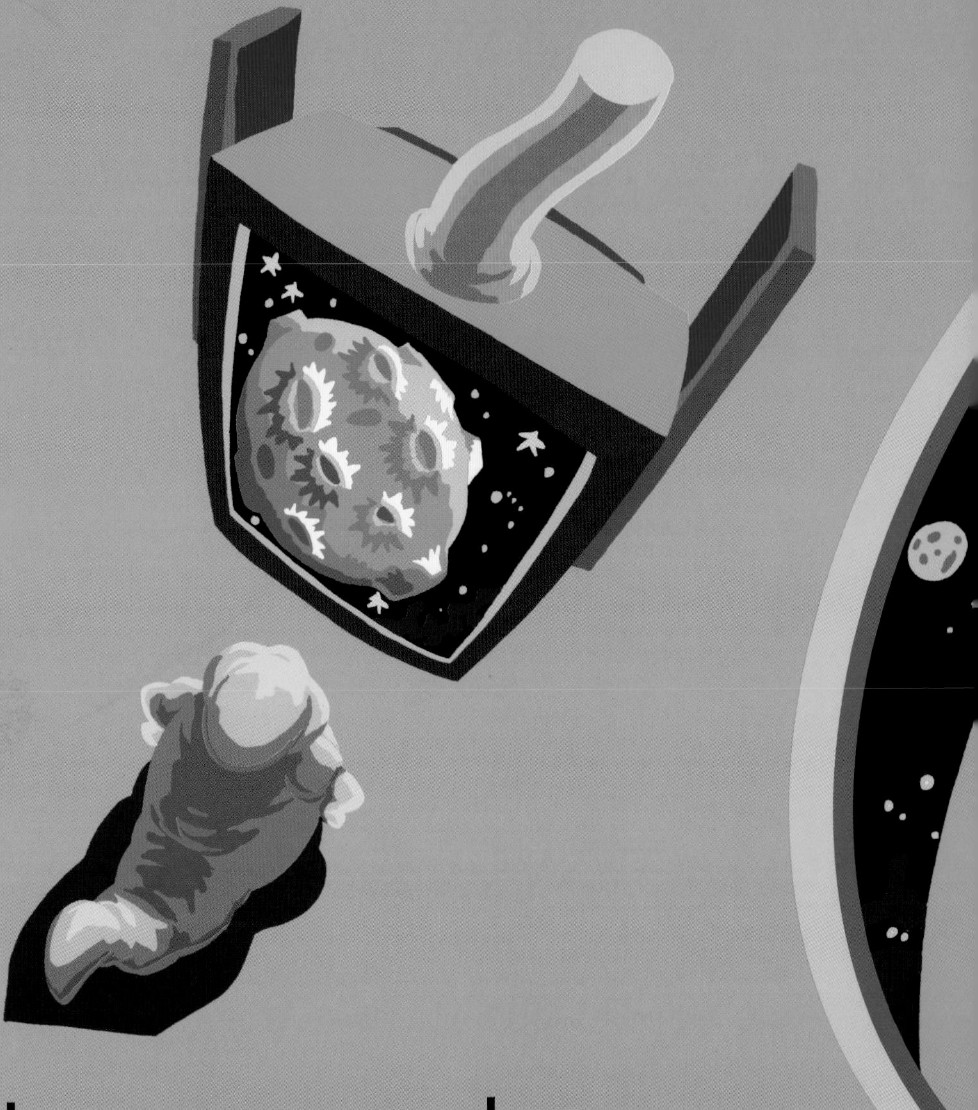

I can see the moon.

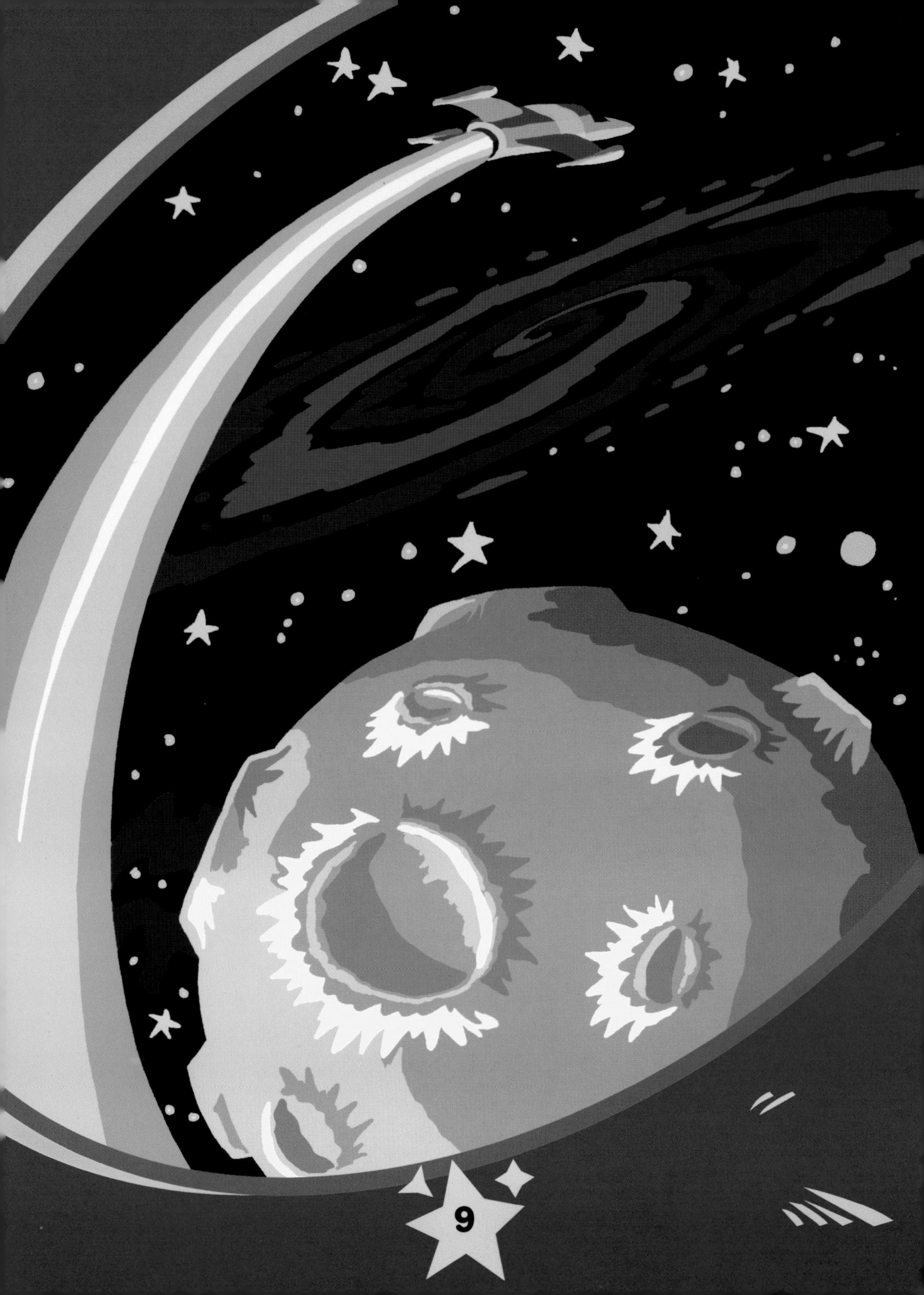

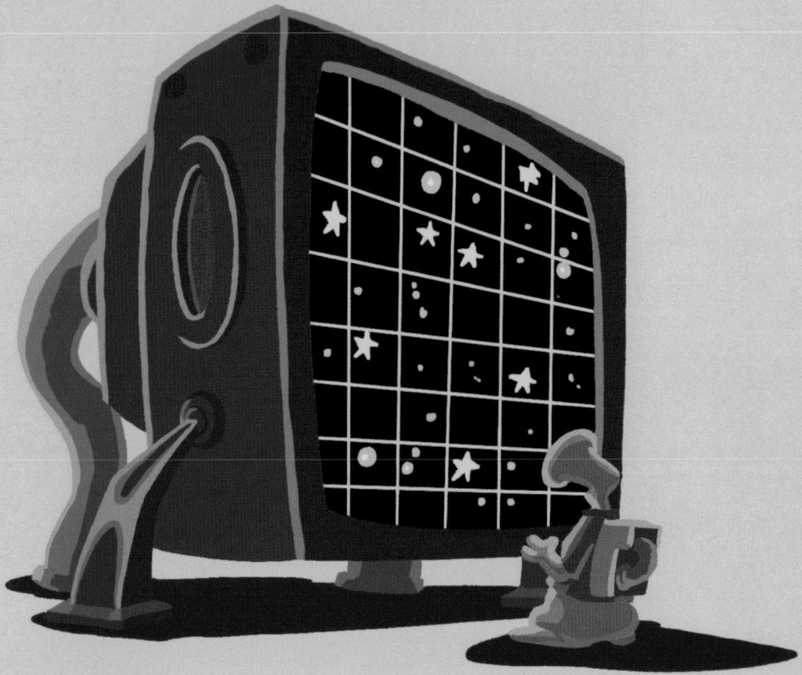

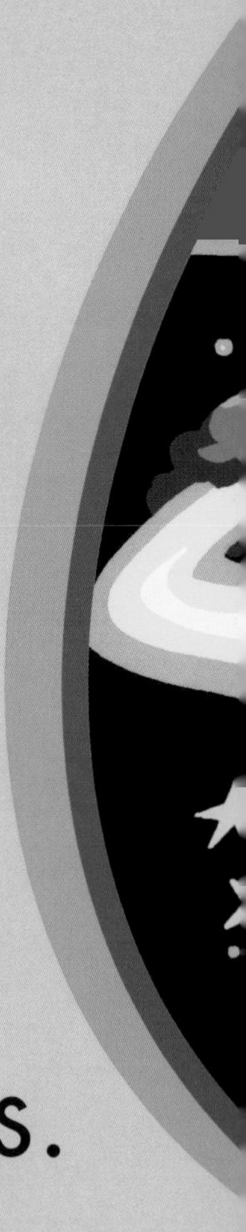

I can see the stars.

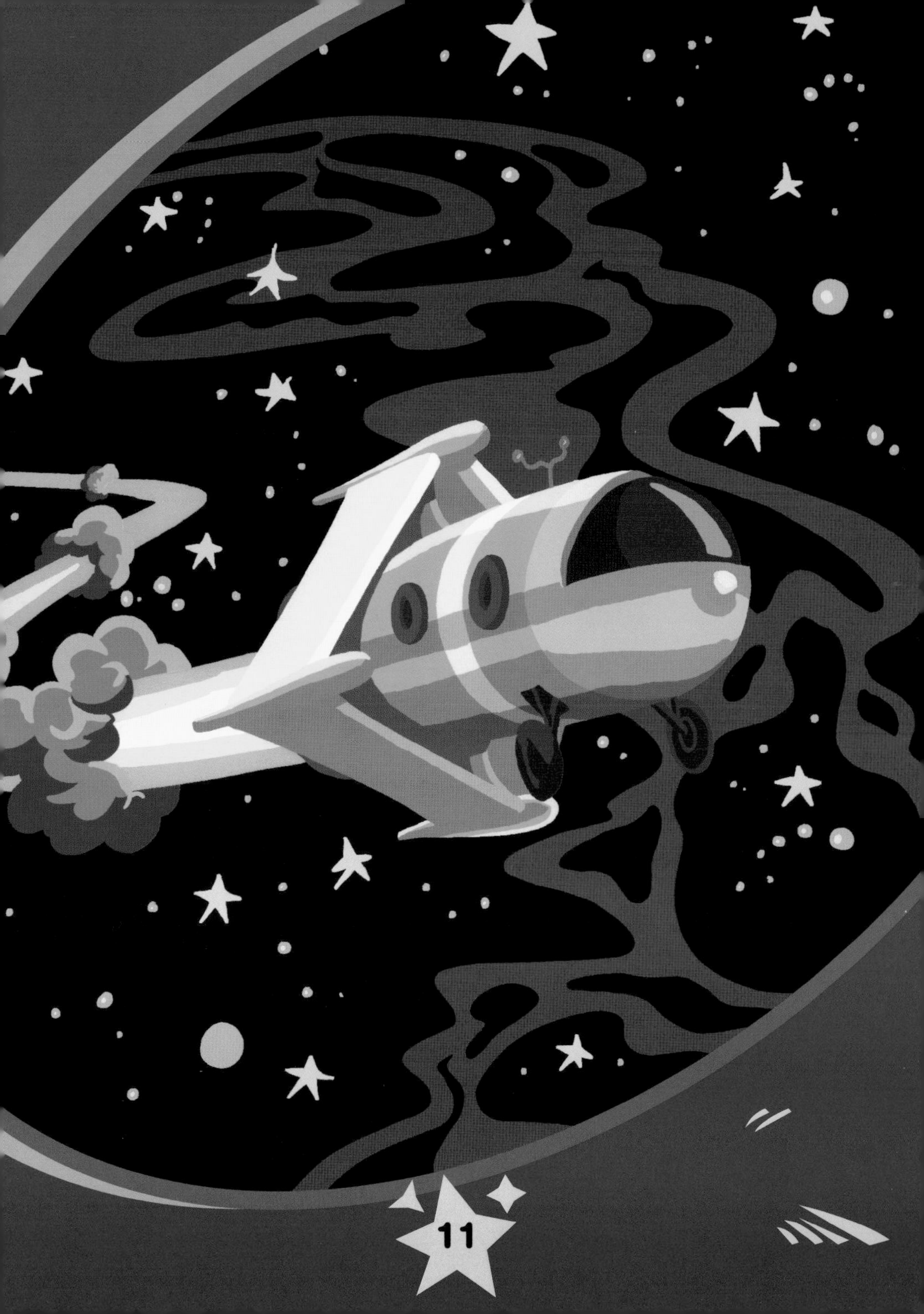

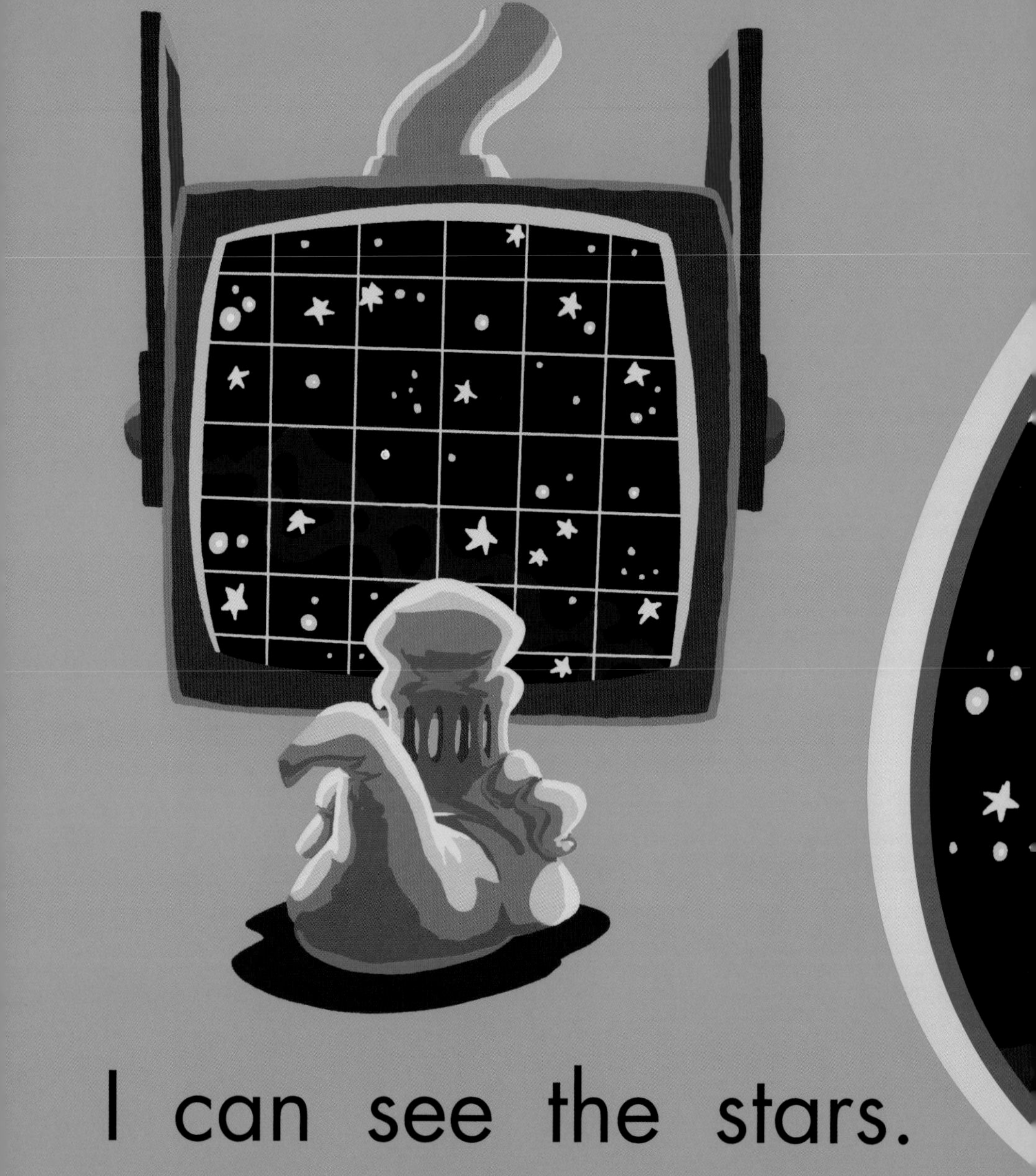

I can see the stars.

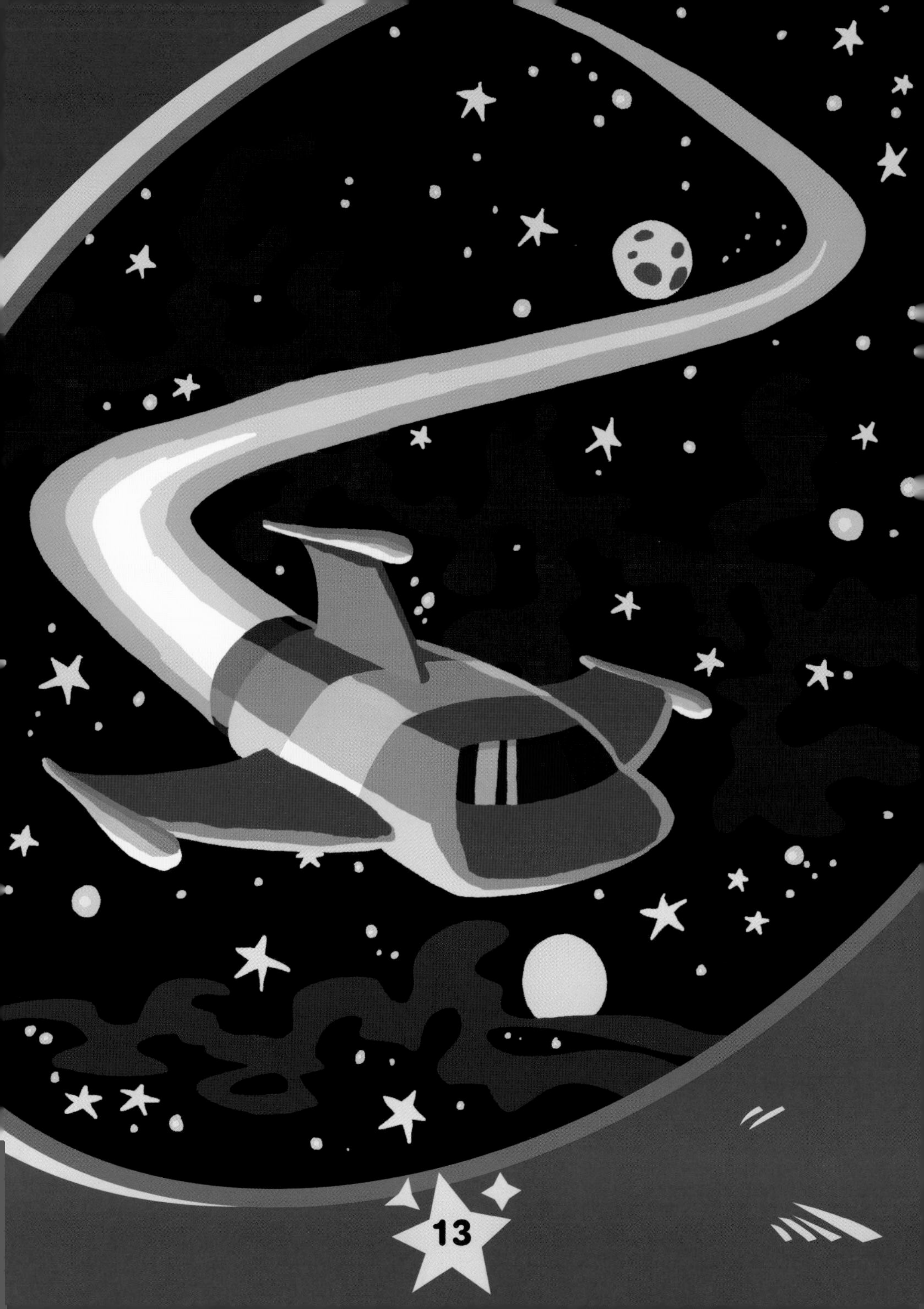

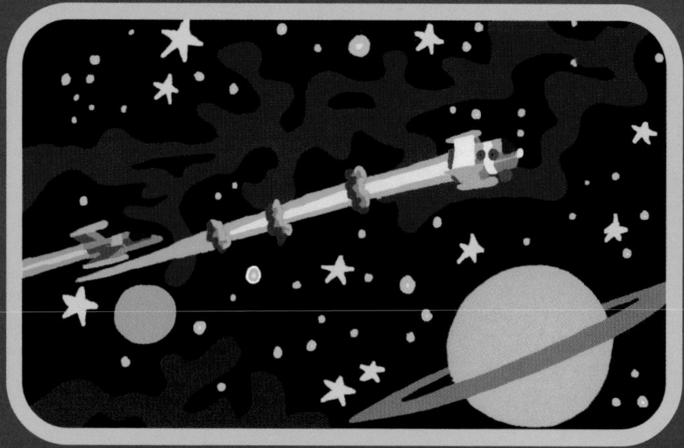

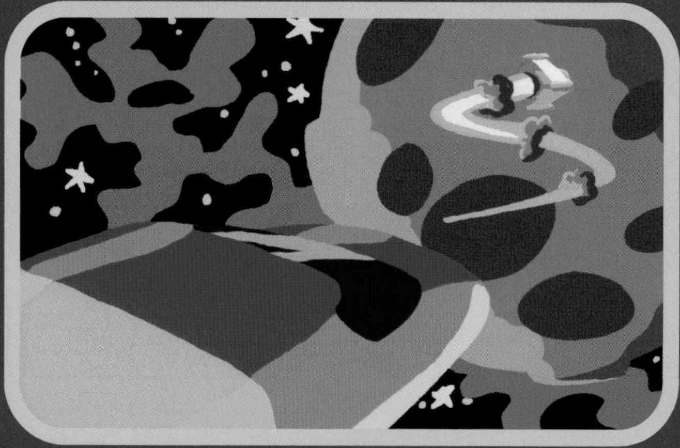

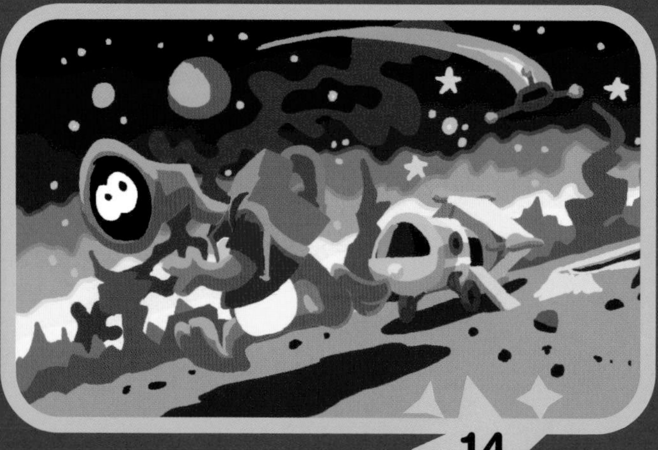

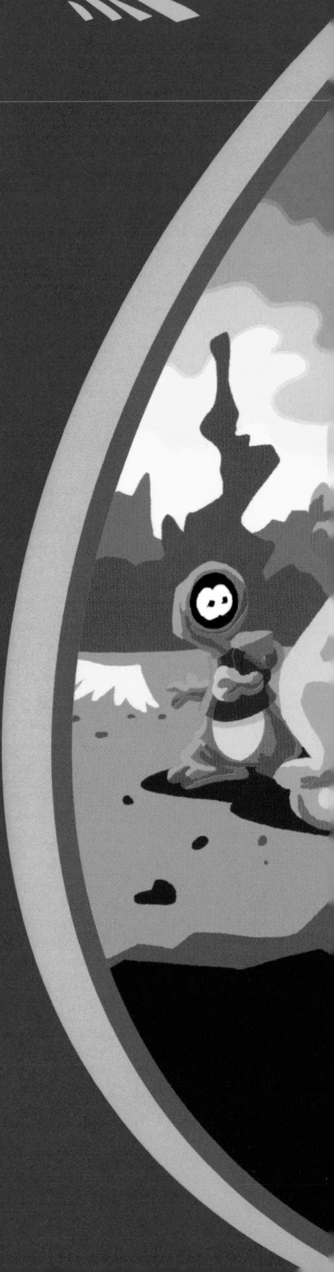

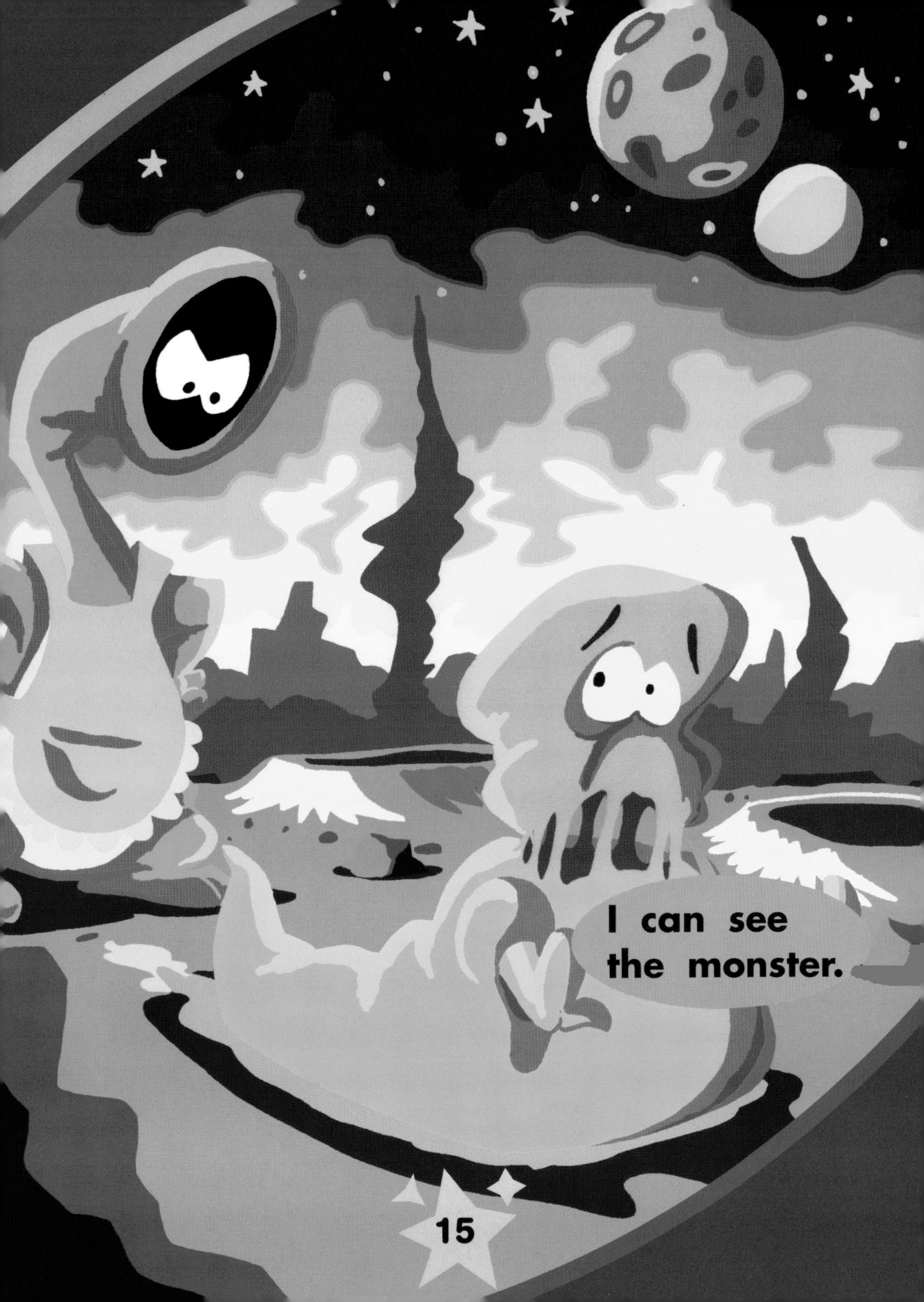
I can see
the monster.

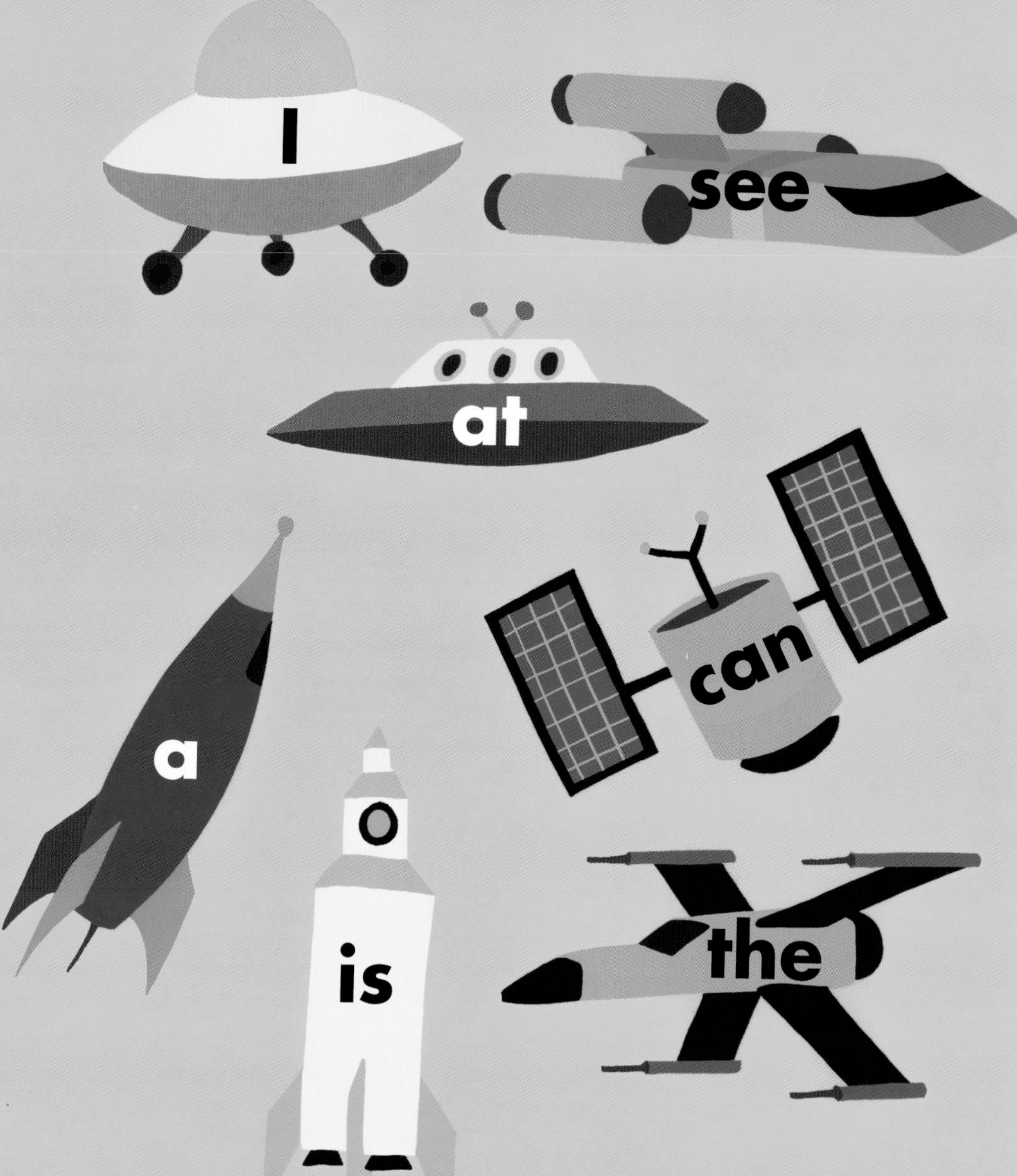
I
see
at
can
a
is
the